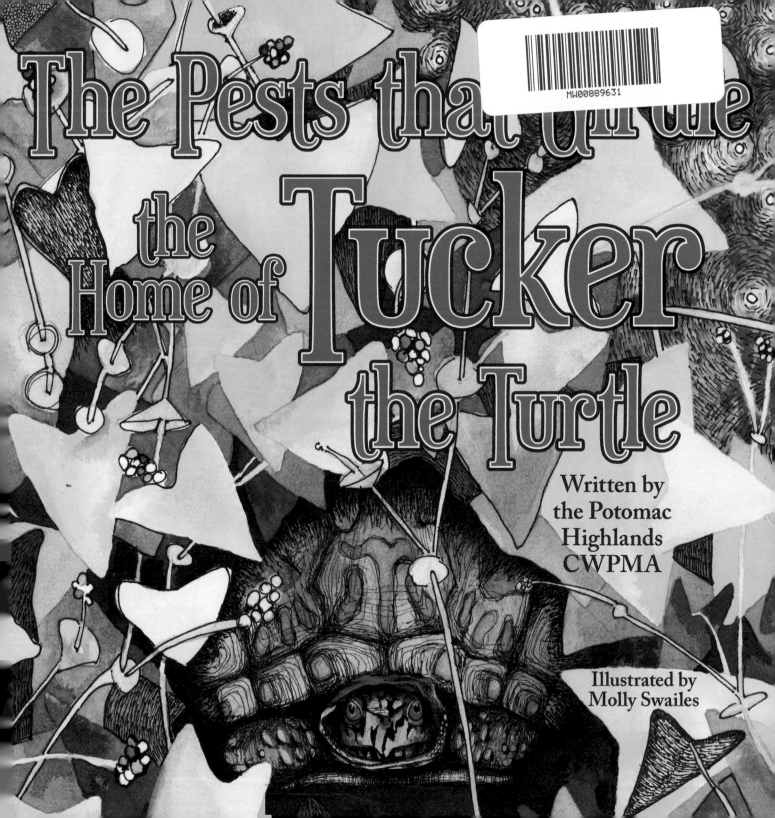

The Pests that untie the Home of Tucker the Turtle

Written by
the Potomac
Highlands
CWPMA

Illustrated by
Molly Swailes

Authors

Cynthia Sandeno
Caroline Dunlap
Traci Hickson
Amy Hill
Rosey Santerre
Brittany Callahan
Steve Niethamer
Rebecca Urbanczyk
Evan Burks

Copyright © 2013 the Potomac Highlands CWPMA
All rights reserved.

ISBN: 1492109525
ISBN 13: 9781492109525

Dedication

This book is in honor of the wild and wonderful natural places that we all love to see,
But it is dedicated to those who protect it – you're as important as can be.

Men and women, boys and girls taking actions great and small,
Those who save our wild habitats, we need you most of all.

We will never give up our battle to provide places for wildlife to roam,
Or critters like Tucker the Turtle, will no longer have a home.

Introduction

My name is Tucker the Turtle, and I live in many places as you will see.
I'd like to share my poems, won't you take a trip with me?

To my home in the forests, rivers, and ponds is where we are bound.
We'll move among the trees and flowers, crawling across the ground.

I'll tell you about the pests I've met and how my home has begun to change,
As non-native invasive species quickly spread across my range.

Garlic Mustard

GARLIC mustard with your lovely white flower, we thought you were delicious,
But when you raided our woods and farms, we realized you were quite vicious!

When I see you growing in the woods along my favorite trail,
I gently pull you from the ground and throw you in my pail.

Mile-A-Minute

WHAT do you call a weed that grows ten inches in two days,
That can pollinate itself and steal most of the sun's rays?

Should you spy a patch of Mile-A-Minute growing in your yard,
Be sure to get it out at once, before it gets too hard!

Snakehead Fish

SNAKEHEAD fish are almost here, they are coming up the bay,
Eating our fish, frogs, and turtles, whatever comes their way.

The snakehead fish is quite delish, and you'll do us all a favor,
If you enjoy a home-cooked meal featuring the snakehead flavor.

Gypsy Moth

Oh, gypsy moth caterpillar, with your dots of blue and red,
You think you are so lovely as you spin your silken thread.

The mighty oaks and other trees tremble when you're in their sights.
You come along with all your friends and greedy appetites.

You eat, you munch, you march along, till all the trees are bare,
Leaving nothing for our forest friends, you laugh, you do not care.

Japanese Knotweed

KNOTWEED with your bamboo stalks, many have fallen for your spell,
I wish the Forest Police would come, and take you off to jail.

There you wouldn't bother our rivers or hurt the native trout,
Wild our mountain streams would be – we've got to keep you out.

Oh, I would be so happy, without seeing your flowers of white,
And fish would swim and jump and play – life would be dynamite.

Chinese Mystery Snail

CHINESE Mystery Snails are new and really quite the issue,
In fact, they carry diseases that can infect your human tissue.

What a shame you can't control this invasive snail with ease,
Since it can close its "trapdoor" whenever it does please.

Tree-of-Heaven

YOU were brought here from China and you quickly had us beat,
Spouting up in many places like the sidewalk and the street.

Your leaves look like our hickories, yet they lack their many teeth,
And at the base a single gland I see from underneath.

I detect the Tree-of-Heaven by its leaves and nasty smell,
And miss the native trees and shrubs it surely will expel.

Emerald Ash Borer

YOUR bullet-shaped body is a stunning, metallic green,
Yet, the way you destroy our native ash is really quite obscene.

First found in Michigan, you've been traveling from state to state,
Destroying millions of ash trees, determining our forests' fate.

If people let you hitch a ride, in their next load of firewood,
They'll help you find your very own, brand new neighborhood.

Hemlock Woolly Adelgid

ODE to the mighty Hemlock, who stands so wild and tall,
A majestic sight you are, standing beside the waterfall,

Providing a home for birds, and plenty of shade for trout,
Now the woolly adelgid, completely wipes you out!

Japanese Stiltgrass

STILTGRASS grows in thick, dense mats and spreads to cover the ground
It likes the sun, it likes the shade, anywhere disturbance is found.

Stiltgrass grows near streams and roads, in fields and even wetlands,
This plant can grow in a variety of soil types, it even grows in sand.

Nothing eats this plant, that's a problem don't you see,
Not rabbits, not deer, not you, and certainly not me!

Asian Longhorned Beetle

I WAS walking through the woods one day when I saw an interesting sight,
Two big beetles whose long antennae were banded black and white.

They turned their heads and looked at me saying, "Hello," with a smile.
"We'd like to start our family here and stay for a long, long while."

"With jaws of steel, we love to kill your maples and other trees,
Which means you'll lose your syrup, and the homes of birds and bees."

"We've traveled around the country, hidden in your firewood.
We shouldn't have been transported, now we're here for good."

Zebra Mussel

YOU showed up in some ballast water dumped in lake St. Clair,
You interfere with native mussels, making life too hard to bear.

You attach to boats, pilings, pipes, and sometimes even turtles.
Native species can't compete, for you put up too many hurdles.

Hydrilla

HYDRILLA decreases oxygen in our favorite ponds and lakes,
Clean your equipment between each trip, do your part for goodness sakes!.

Moving water, still water, warm water, cold,
Hydrilla grows in all these types, it really is too bold.

Purple Loosestrife

BEAUTIFUL flowers of purple, can they really be that bad?
Just ask the ducks and geese about the wetlands they once had.

We wanted color in our garden, that's why we brought you here,
Not knowing you produced a million seeds, in a single growing year.

Purple loosestrife will spread quickly and you are sure to expand,
Taking over all of our precious, native, wetlands.

Kudzu

FORMING a great green blanket that covers fields and many trees,
Kudzu smothers all the branches, like a python from Burmese.

Growing three feet in a single day, you really are a horror,
Our trees don't have a chance between you and the ash borer!